Names: Colbert, Autumn Grey, author. | Zelenkevich, Sasha, illustrator.
Title: I love you more than you know / Autumn Grey Colbert; Sasha Zelenkevich.
Description: Logan, UT: Plum Coconut, 2023. | Summary: A bedtime story meant to calm,
soothe, and support children.
Identifiers: LCCN: 2023923098 | ISBN: 978-1-955591-16-4 (hardcover) | 978-1-955591-13-3 (board) |
978-1-955591-14-0 (paperback) | 978-1-955591-15-7 (ebook)
Subjects: LCSH Mother and child–Juvenile fiction. | Bedtime–Juvenile fiction. | BISAC JUVENILE FICTION
/ Family / General | JUVENILE FICTION / Bedtime & Dreams
Classification: LCC PZ7.1 .C65 Il 2023 | DDC [E]–dc23

I LOVE YOU
MORE THAN
YOU
KNOW

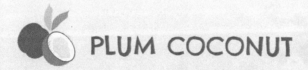

PLUM COCONUT

ILLUSTRATIONS: Sasha Zelenkevich

My darling little one,
I love you more than you know.

It is my greatest honor
to care for you and watch
you learn and grow.

Each day with you is unique,
filled with laughter and play.

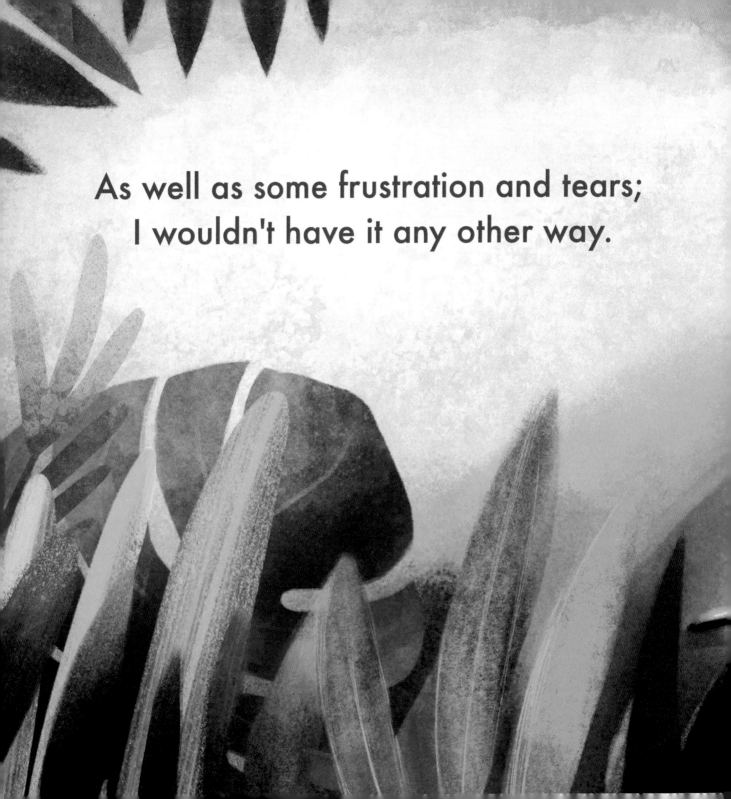

As well as some frustration and tears;
I wouldn't have it any other way.

There is nothing in this world
you could say or do,

that would ever change
my endless love for you.

I can't wait to get to know you better as you get older.

As your interests shine through,

and you get stronger and bolder.

You are my sweetheart,
my love, my sunshine.

I can feel the warmth of my love spread to your heart from mine.

When I think of you,
it makes my heart glow.

Just remember, I'll always
love you more than you know.

Dedicated to my Willow ♥

Made in the USA
Las Vegas, NV
02 March 2024